Princess Ellie's Moonlight Mystery

Ellie felt blissfully happy as she rode along. This was how camping should be – just like in her book. If only it could always be this good. If only there wasn't another night to get through; another night when the mysterious creature might come back to get them.

Look out for more sparkly adventures of

The Pony-Mad Princess!

Princess Ellie to the Rescue

Princess Ellie's Secret

A Puzzle for Princess Ellie

Princess Ellie's Starlight Adventure

A Surprise for Princess Ellie

Princess Ellie's Holiday Adventure

Princess Ellie and the Palace Plot

Princess Ellie's Christmas

Princess Ellie Saves the Day

Princess Ellie's Summer Holiday

Princess Ellie's Treasure Hunt

Princess Ellie's Perfect Plan

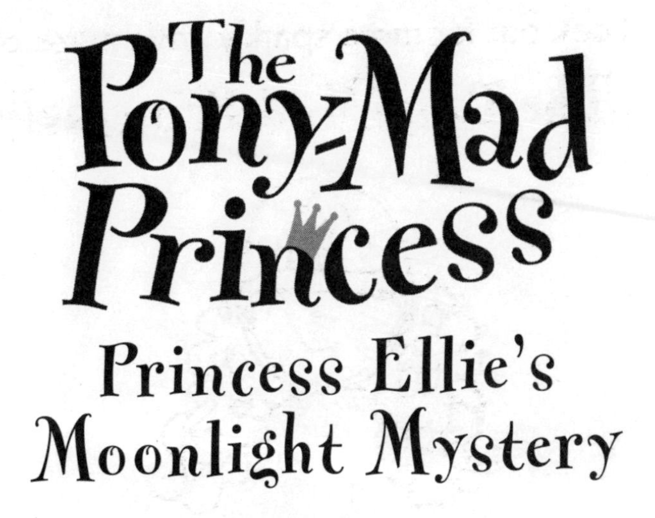

Diana Kimpton

Illustrated by Lizzie Finlay

For Rebecca

This edition first published in 2014 by Usborne Publishing Ltd.,
Usborne House, 83-85 Saffron Hill, London EC1N 8RT, England.
www.usborne.com

First published in 2004. Based on an original concept by Anne Finnis.

A CIP catalogue record for this book is available from the British Library.

ISBN 9781409566007 JFMA JJASOND/14 01427/4

Printed in Chatham, Kent, UK.

Chapter 1

"They said 'yes'!" yelled Princess Ellie as she ran into the yard. Her frothy pink dress looked ridiculous with her wellington boots. But she didn't care. She was in too much of a hurry to share her good news.

"That's brilliant," said her best friend, Kate. She bounced with excitement, sending the water slopping over the edge

of the bucket she was carrying.

Meg, the palace groom, put a bulging haynet beside Moonbeam's door. "I'm really pleased for you. But I must admit I'm surprised. I didn't think the King and Queen would approve of you going camping."

"Neither did I," said Kate. She dumped the bucket beside the haynet and undid the bolt on the door. Moonbeam poked her head out to see what was happening. She spotted Ellie immediately and whickered a welcome.

Ellie grinned and stroked the palomino's nose. "They didn't like the idea at first," she explained. "But the Prime Minister persuaded them it would do me good. I'll be perfectly safe in the palace grounds and he thinks it will be character forming, whatever that means."

"I think it'll be fun," laughed Kate, as she swung Moonbeam's door open and carried the bucket inside.

"So do I," said Ellie. She picked up the haynet and followed her friend into the stable.

Moonbeam immediately started pulling out pieces of hay. She made the net bounce and jiggle so much that it was hard to tie it to the ring on the wall.

Kate pushed the hungry pony away so Ellie could finish quickly. Then she grabbed Ellie by the arm and pulled her impatiently towards the door. "Come on," she said. "I've got something really exciting to show you."

"Can't it wait?" asked Ellie. "We've got so much to plan."

"There's loads of time to do that," replied Kate. "You've got to see this first."

Ellie was intrigued. What could be more exciting than planning their camping trip? She followed her friend round the back of the palace, past the garages and storerooms, until they reached the workshop. Kate's grandad was waiting for them there. He was the palace handyman and this was his special place.

As soon as he opened the door, Ellie saw what the secret was. Two tiny lambs tottered

towards them, bleating loudly. "They're so cute," she said, as she kneeled down on the dusty floor. The boldest lamb came forward and sucked one of her fingers.

"They're hungry," said Kate's grandad. "You're just in time to give them these." He handed Kate and Ellie a feeding bottle each, full of warm milk.

The lambs immediately started to suck hungrily. Ellie was surprised how hard they pulled. She had to hold the bottle tightly to stop it being tugged right out of her hands.

"Why have *you* got them?" she asked. "I thought the shepherd at the farm looked after all the sheep."

"He does," laughed Kate's grandad. "And they keep him very busy. That's why I'm giving him a hand with these two."

"Grandad's great with orphaned animals," explained Kate. "He's reared loads of lambs before and some kittens, and even a deer."

Kate's grandad smiled. "That was my Stanley," he explained. "I found him when he was a tiny fawn. He must have been in an accident. He'd been badly hurt."

"Grandad nursed him back to health," interrupted Kate, who had obviously heard the story many times before.

"Not quite," said her grandad. "His left ear never stood up properly again. It

drooped sideways and made him look a real character. Which he was, of course. He's not at all timid like a normal deer."

"What happened to him?" asked Ellie. "Did you keep him as a pet?"

The old man shook his head. "You can't keep a wild animal cooped up. It isn't right. When he was big enough, I let him go free in the deer park." He stared out of the window and smiled. "That was over two years ago now, but I still see him sometimes when I'm out there."

Ellie fed the last few drops of milk to the lamb. It was sleepy now that its stomach was full, so she cradled it in her arms, delighting in the soft warmth of its body. "My parents

say we can go camping," she announced, proudly. "We're going to take two of my ponies with us. I got the idea from one of my books."

"It's going to be brilliant," said Kate. "Two whole nights away from home."

"Two whole nights of total freedom," added Ellie with such enthusiasm that the lamb woke up. "No rules, no servants, no nothing."

Kate's grandad smiled and raised his eyebrows. "And you both know all about camping, do you?"

Ellie hesitated. There was something in his voice that suggested he didn't think they did. But she'd read a book about it. She must know enough. "I'm going to talk to Dad about the arrangements later," she said, confidently.

"Then we'd better start planning," said Kate. She pulled some paper and a pencil

from a shelf and started to write a list of equipment. "I know what we need because I've been camping lots of times with Mum and Dad." Kate's dad worked abroad building roads and bridges, while Kate stayed with her grandparents so she didn't have to keep changing schools.

"But that was in other countries," said Ellie. "The palace grounds are different. They're not like the jungle, or the desert."

"That's true," agreed Kate, crossing mosquito nets off the list. "But we still need tents, and sleeping bags and pit latrines."

"Pit what?" asked Ellie.

"Latrines," said Kate. "They're holes in the ground. For you know..."

"What?" asked Ellie in confusion.

"Toilets," hissed Kate, and then collapsed in giggles.

Ellie gulped. Her book hadn't mentioned anything about that. Maybe camping was going to be harder than she'd expected.

Chapter 2

By the time they had finished planning, Ellie was late for the meeting with her father. She raced back to the palace at top speed and burst into his office, brandishing the list. Then she stopped in dismay. Sitting next to the King was her governess, Miss Stringle. They were both staring at her in disapproval.

"Just look at the state of your clothes,

Aurelia," said the King.

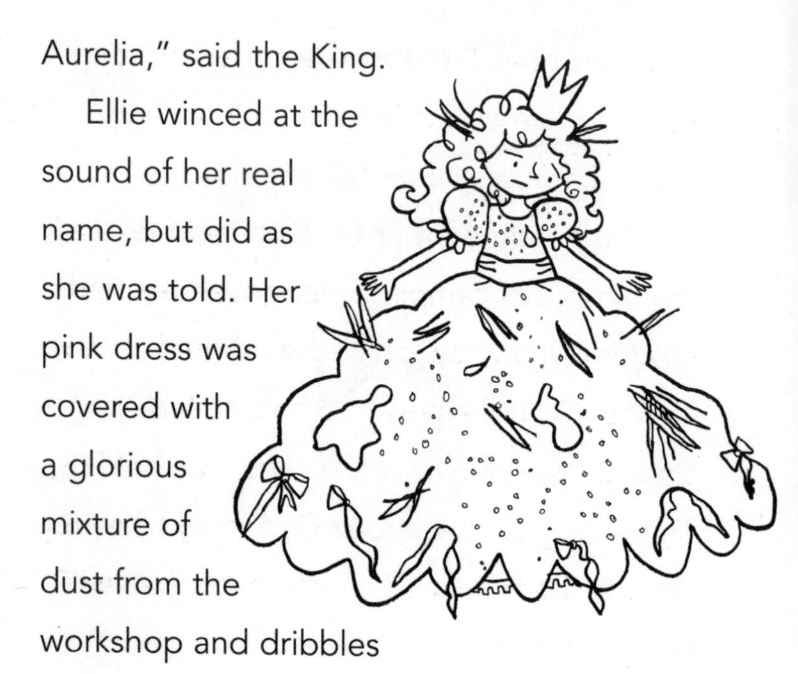

Ellie winced at the sound of her real name, but did as she was told. Her pink dress was covered with a glorious mixture of dust from the workshop and dribbles of milk. There were pieces of hay stuck to its frills and several of its ribbon bows had come undone. "I'm sorry," she said, as convincingly as she could. "I've been busy feeding a lamb and making plans for the camp."

The King sighed, and glanced at his watch. "There's no time for you to get

changed now. I'm due in another meeting soon, so I've asked Miss Stringle to help make the arrangements."

Ellie groaned inwardly. This could take all the fun out of camping. Her governess had strict ideas on how princesses should behave.

Miss Stringle stood up and leafed through the pile of papers she was holding. Then she coughed politely, curtseyed to the King and announced, "I estimate that we'll need eight tents."

"*Eight!* What for?" asked Ellie. "We only need two – one for us and one for the ponies."

"Nonsense," declared Miss Stringle. "You're a princess. You can't possibly share a tent with someone who isn't royal."

Ellie glared at her angrily. "But Kate's my best friend," she argued. "I'd be lonely without her."

"That's a very good point," said the King. "And one less tent. So who are the others for?"

Miss Stringle counted on her fingers as she reeled off the names. "There's Princess Aurelia's personal maid to tidy her tent, a cook to prepare the food, a footman to serve the meals, a groom to care for the ponies..."

"No, no, no," Ellie interrupted, crossly. "Camping is about freedom and doing everything ourselves. We don't need servants and we *definitely* don't need a groom. Kate and I can look after the ponies."

"...and a scullery maid to wash the dishes," continued Miss Stringle, taking no notice of the interruption.

"We don't need her either," said Ellie in a voice too loud to ignore. She had never washed up in her life, but she was determined to make her own rules for the camping trip.

The King took the papers from Miss Stringle and read them thoughtfully. "I admire you for wanting to do everything the hard way," he told Ellie, with a mischievous glint in his eye. "So you obviously won't want this portable flushing toilet that Miss Stringle has mistakenly ordered." He picked up a pencil and went to cross the offending item off the list.

Thoughts of pit latrines rushed through Ellie's head and she leaped forward to stop him. "You can leave that if you like."

The King smiled. "That's good to hear. Now let's see if we can work out some other compromises."

Miss Stringle stared at her list thoughtfully. "I suppose we could do without the scullery maid, if we tell the footman to wash up."

"No," said Ellie. "We want to do it all."

"But you can't possibly put up the tents yourselves," argued Miss Stringle. "They're much too heavy for a princess to carry."

"Okay," agreed Ellie, reluctantly. "I don't mind someone else doing that. But only on condition that they go home afterwards."

"That seems reasonable enough," agreed the King.

"But you're not to do any cooking," insisted Miss Stringle. "That would be much too undignified for a princess and we can't risk burns so far from home. I will arrange for all your meals to be sent up from the palace."

"Can't we even make our own breakfast?"

pleaded Ellie. "That's not difficult."

"You can take cornflakes and milk," said the King. "But I agree with Miss Stringle about the danger from fires. We'll send up the hot water for washing."

"We won't need *that*," said Ellie. "The children in my book fetched their water from the stream, and we're going to do the same."

The King looked at her doubtfully. "If that's what you want. But I suspect you're not going to enjoy camping as much as you think."

"Neither do I, Your Majesty," agreed Miss Stringle. "It's really not a suitable activity for a princess."

"Yes, it *is*," said Ellie. "I'm going to be away for a whole weekend and I'm going to love every minute of it."

"If you don't, you can always come back early," sighed the King. "I'm sure you won't manage two whole nights in a tent."

Ellie glared at him. She was sure he was wrong. He must be. How could freedom not be fun?

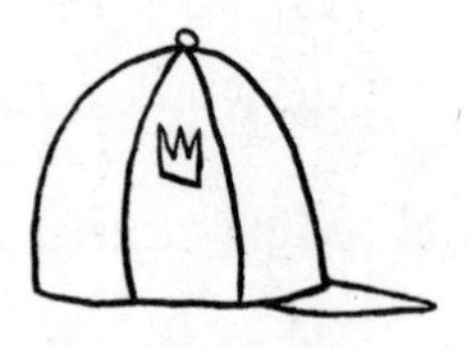

Chapter 3

Ellie's excitement grew all week. She found it even harder than usual to concentrate on her lessons. She didn't want to think of anything except the camping trip.

It was easy to decide which ponies to take. Moonbeam and Rainbow were the obvious choices. Shadow the Shetland was too small, Sundance was too good at escaping and

Starlight, the newest arrival, wasn't fit enough to be ridden very much yet.

Choosing a campsite was more difficult. Miss Stringle wanted it close to the palace, while Ellie wanted it as far away as possible. Neither of them would change their minds, until Meg discovered the perfect spot, a pretty clearing in the woods on the other side of the deer park. Ellie and Kate fell in love with the dappled sunshine and the babbling stream as soon as they saw them, and even Miss Stringle had to agree it was a good choice. It was far enough from the palace to be private, but close enough for the food still to be hot when it arrived.

At long last, Friday came. The last waving lesson of the week was over, and it was time to set out for the campsite. Ellie and Kate

mounted Moonbeam and Rainbow, and everyone came to see them off. Even the servants were leaning out of the palace windows, waving goodbye.

Meg gave the girls a large envelope containing a treasure hunt to keep them busy on Saturday. Kate's gran, the palace cook, gave them food for midnight feasts. Even Miss Stringle gave them a gift-wrapped present.

"It's pencils and paper," she explained. "In case you want to write an essay while you're away."

"Is she mad?" whispered Kate.

"No," replied Ellie, pushing the unopened parcel to the bottom of her backpack. "She's a teacher. She always wants to spoil everything by making me write about it."

The King and Queen were the last to say their farewells. They had put on their second-best crowns to mark the importance of the occasion. The Queen looked worried as she kissed Ellie goodbye. "I do hope you enjoy it," she said.

"But I don't expect you will," added the King. He handed Ellie a mobile phone in a red velvet case embroidered with the royal crest. "Call us when you've had

enough, and we'll come and bring you home."

"I won't need it," declared Ellie. She thrust the phone into her backpack, tucking it firmly under Miss Stringle's parcel. "This is going to be the best weekend of my whole life. I'll see you on Sunday when we get back."

Moonbeam seemed to share her excitement and was eager to be on the move. She tossed her head as Ellie shortened the reins, sending her snow-white mane cascading in all directions.

"This is going to be fantastic," said Kate, as she rode up beside her on Rainbow.

After one last wave at everyone, they trotted out of the stable yard and away from the palace. It was a route they often

took when they went for a ride. But today it felt different. Today it was leading them to an adventure.

As they turned into the deer park, Ellie looked back. The Queen was still there, waving her handkerchief. For the first time, Ellie realized how strange it was going to be at bedtime when there was no one to kiss her goodnight. But she pushed the thought away and concentrated on the pleasure of riding.

Although they were keen to reach the campsite, they decided not to go there by the shortest route. Riding the long way

round would make it feel further away and more of an adventure. It would also let the ponies burn off their surplus energy before they settled down for the night.

They cantered along the edge of the deer park. Then they slowed to a walk and turned onto a path that zig-zagged its way up the hillside. It was so narrow that the bracken on either side swished against their legs. Moonbeam grabbed some as she went past. The leaves were too big to fit in her mouth, so they hung out either side.

"You're nearly as greedy as Shadow," laughed Ellie, as she leaned forward and pulled out the leaves from between the pony's teeth.

The path grew wider when they reached the wood, so they started to trot. Dappled

sunlight shone between the branches, and the ponies' hooves made hardly any sound on the soft ground. Ellie's excitement grew and grew as each step took them closer to the campsite.

At long last, they reached the edge of the trees and rode out into the sunshine. Then they stopped and stared in surprise.

"Wow!" said Kate. "I've never seen a tent like that before."

Neither had Ellie. The tent on the front of her book had been made of sensible green canvas. This one was neither sensible nor green. It was bright pink and decorated with gold bows and embroidered gold crowns. Miniature versions of the royal flag

fluttered at each end. Even the ropes that held it up were made of golden cord.

"I'm sorry," laughed Ellie. "Miss Stringle never mentioned this."

Fortunately, her governess had left the horsey part of the arrangements to Meg, so the pony shelter was made of simple white canvas. It was large and airy, with

a roof to protect Moonbeam and Rainbow from the rain, and three sides to protect them from the wind. The fourth side was open to make sure they had plenty of light.

Ellie felt very proud as she led Moonbeam inside. It was the first time she and Kate had ever been completely responsible for the ponies by themselves. They quickly unsaddled them, put on their headcollars and tied them to the rope that ran along the back of the shelter. Then they left the ponies munching their hay while they went to fetch water.

They couldn't resist exploring the pink tent on the way. The inside was nearly as grand as the outside. The roof was lined with gold silk and embroidered with silver stars. There was pink satin ribbon wound

round the tent poles and the floor was covered with pink carpet.

To Ellie's relief, Miss Stringle had remembered that she wanted to sleep on the ground. So there were no four-poster camp beds, just two sleeping bags – one on each side of the tent. At the far end, stood a packet of cornflakes and a carton of milk, ready for the morning.

The most exciting thing of all was that there wasn't an adult in sight. They really were free to do as they pleased. "This is brilliant," said Ellie, as she picked up her bucket and headed for the stream.

Even fetching the water was more exciting than using a tap. The stream bubbled over rocks and down a tiny waterfall into a wide, shallow pool with

stepping stones across it. It was such a good place to play that they stayed much longer than they needed to.

The sun was low in the sky by the time they carried their full buckets back to camp.

The tents looked peaceful in the evening sunlight. But as soon as they reached the pony shelter, they realized that something was horribly wrong. Moonbeam's headcollar was still tied to the rope, but her head wasn't in it any more. The palomino pony had disappeared.

Chapter 4

Ellie looked around desperately, but there was no sign of Moonbeam. She bent down and picked up the empty headcollar. "It's still done up. She must have wriggled it over her ears."

"Do you think she's gone home?" asked Kate.

"I hope not," groaned Ellie. "Everyone will laugh at us if she has."

Suddenly, there was a noise from the bright

pink tent. Ellie and Kate raced over and lifted the door flap. Just inside was a creamy coloured rump and a snow-white tail.

Moonbeam's head was deep inside the cornflakes packet as she happily munched its contents.

"That's our breakfast!" shouted Kate.

"She'll have our midnight feast as well if we don't get her out soon," said Ellie. She tried to squeeze into the tent past Moonbeam's backside. But the pony whisked her tail and raised a hoof in warning.

"Watch out in case she kicks!" called Kate.

"Ponies never like being disturbed while they're eating," said Ellie, backing

quickly out of the tent.

"But we can't just leave her till she's finished," said Kate.

The obvious solution was to go in another way. But a quick search soon showed that there wasn't one. Miss Stringle had thought of everything they might need, except a back door.

"Good girl," called Ellie in a soothing voice, as she braced herself for a second attempt at rescuing their supplies. The palomino pony stopped munching and listened. As Ellie tried to squeeze past, she put a reassuring hand on Moonbeam's rump and said, "It's only me." The pony flicked her ears and whisked her tail again, but she didn't kick.

Ellie moved quickly along Moonbeam's side and grabbed hold of her mane. Then she put the headcollar rope around the pony's

neck to stop her escaping while she tried to prise her head out of the cornflakes packet.

Moonbeam didn't make that an easy task. She was determined to eat as much as possible while she still had the chance. She stepped sideways, trying to push Ellie away. In the process, her hoof landed on the milk carton, crushing it completely and spraying milk in all directions.

Ellie grabbed hold of the cornflakes packet with her free hand and pulled so hard that it tore open. Golden flakes spilled down to join the puddle of milk on the floor. Moonbeam pushed her head down to try to eat them, but Ellie was too quick for her. She slipped on the headcollar and buckled it into place.

"Now we just have to get her outside," said Ellie.

Kate peered in through the entrance. "I don't think there's room to turn her around," she groaned.

"Can we get her out backwards?" asked Ellie.

Kate looked doubtful. "Only if she goes absolutely straight."

Ellie sighed. "We'll have to try. There's no other way." She urged Moonbeam to walk backwards. The pony obeyed unwillingly. She was still trying to reach the last of the cornflakes.

"Careful," called Kate. "She's swinging too much to the left."

Ellie tried again. One step. Two steps...

Suddenly, Moonbeam's back foot landed on an automatic umbrella Miss Stringle had provided. It triggered the release button and the umbrella unfolded with a loud whoosh.

The sudden movement terrified Moonbeam. Before Ellie could stop her, the pony lurched forward, cannoned into the back wall of the tent and swung round.

Kate was right. There wasn't room for Moonbeam to turn. Her hindquarters smashed into the rear tent pole, cracking it in two. The top half of the pole crashed down, hitting the pony as it fell. The shock sent Moonbeam into an even greater panic. As the roof of the tent collapsed around her, she hurtled for the entrance.

Luckily, she got through first time. Ellie tore after her, half running and half dragged, as she hung on desperately to the rope. She was determined not to let Moonbeam disappear again.

Moonbeam stopped by the edge of the

clearing. Ellie and Kate stroked her face and spoke to her soothingly until she settled down and started to graze.

Then they looked at the tent in dismay. It was a total disaster. One end had collapsed completely, so the roof was lying on the ground. The other end was still vaguely upright, but it wouldn't take much of a wind to bring it down. There was no way they could sleep in it like that.

Chapter 5

"I don't want to go home," wailed Kate as they tied Moonbeam up in the pony shelter, making sure her headcollar was tight enough this time.

"Neither do I," sighed Ellie. Most of all, she didn't want to phone her father and admit that something had already gone wrong. The thought of the King saying, "I told you so,"

filled her with fresh determination. "It's only a broken pole. We must be able to fix *that*."

They went back to the damaged tent and crawled inside. Ellie struggled to her feet, lifting the collapsed roof high above her head.

"That's better," laughed Kate. "If you can

just stand there for the next two days, everything will be fine."

"Don't be daft," giggled Ellie. "Just grab the bits of pole and get out of here." She held up the roof until Kate was

safely through the entrance. Then she let go and ran outside as the tent collapsed again.

They unwound the pink ribbon from the pole and used it to lash the broken pieces together. It didn't work. The joint was so wobbly that they had to undo it all and start again.

Suddenly, Ellie had an idea. She rummaged in her backpack and pulled out the unopened parcel from Miss Stringle. "Maybe this is going to be more useful than we thought," said Ellie, as she unwrapped it.

Inside were several sheets of writing paper and two pencils. Ellie pulled out the paper and wound it tightly round the join in the pole.

Then she placed the pencils either side to act like a splint, added a layer of gaily coloured wrapping paper, and tied everything tightly together with the ribbon. This time the joint didn't wobble.

Back in the tent, Ellie lifted up the roof again while Kate carefully eased the pole into position. Then Ellie let go and they both held their breath as the pole took the full weight of the material.

"Yippee!" shrieked Kate, as the mended pole stood straight and tall. Their repair had worked.

"We're brilliant," said Ellie. "We can handle anything."

Their celebrations were cut short by the sound of an engine. They ran outside just in time to see the royal Range Rover arrive.

Higginbottom, the butler, stepped down from the driver's seat and bowed. "His Majesty asked me to check that everything is all right, Your Highness." He looked completely out of place in his evening suit and white gloves.

"Everything's fine," Ellie replied, quickly. She crossed her fingers behind her back, hoping he wouldn't spot that the tent looked much tattier than when he put it up. Several of the gold bows had come untied in the chaos and one of the royal flags had fallen off completely.

To Ellie's relief, he didn't seem to notice. Neither did the footmen who were unloading huge silver trays with matching silver covers.

"Supper!" cried Ellie with delight. Her tummy felt so empty that she was tempted to start eating immediately. But she didn't. She waited until Higginbottom had driven away. She didn't want her feeling of freedom spoiled by having servants around.

Kate's gran obviously understood the needs of hungry campers. The trays held plates piled

high with roast chicken, mashed potato and lashings of gravy.

By the time they had finished eating it, the sun had set completely. They had to switch on their torches so they could see well enough to eat their syrup sponge and custard.

Ellie was glad the food was hot. The warmth of the day had vanished with the sun and she was feeling chilly. "It's a shame we can't have a campfire. The children in my book all sit round a fire and sing songs after supper."

"We can still sing," suggested Kate. "We did that every night when I camped in the desert with Mum and Dad." She paused as a large raindrop landed on her nose, and added, "But it didn't rain there."

Ellie watched in dismay as more drops

spattered into her pudding bowl. "It didn't rain in my book either," she grumbled.

Then the clouds burst, releasing a deluge of water. The girls rushed into the tent and gazed out, waiting for it to stop. But it didn't. Instead, it settled into a steady downpour that was obviously going to last for ages.

The gloomy weather made the girls feel gloomy too. Neither of them felt like singing now. "Let's go to bed," suggested Ellie. "Maybe it'll be better in the morning."

But even going to bed was harder than she expected. First, there was the run through the rain and dark to the portable toilet. Then, there was another wet run to the pony shelter, to check on Moonbeam and Rainbow.

Finally, there was the problem of the nightdress. Kate was lucky; she didn't have

one. Instead, she had sensible pony-print pyjamas. But Ellie had a ridiculously frilly pink nightdress made for a princess in a four-poster bed. It was definitely not designed for getting into a sleeping bag. Ellie slid her feet into her bag and tried to wriggle down. But the nightdress refused to slide with her. She ended up with it wrapped round her neck like a frilly scarf.

She clambered out and tried again. The same thing happened. On her third attempt, she gripped the

bottom of the nightdress tightly between her knees. This made sliding somewhat tricky, but it worked. Finally, both Ellie and the nightdress were *inside* the sleeping bag. By then, Kate was already curled up snugly in hers, and nearly asleep.

"Goodnight," whispered Ellie, as she switched off her torch. The night seemed much darker in the tent than it did at the palace. It was certainly colder, and definitely damper.

Ellie wriggled around trying to get comfortable on the hard ground. Perhaps she shouldn't have turned down the camp bed that Miss Stringle had offered. At this rate, she was going to be awake all night. But eventually the pattering of the rain on the tent acted like a lullaby and she drifted off to sleep.

She woke suddenly. For a moment, she wondered where she was. Then she heard the sound that had woken her. Ellie's eyes snapped open in fear. There was something outside – something that was snuffling along the edge of the tent, trying to get in!

Chapter 6

Ellie froze as the snuffling grew closer and closer. Now the creature was just the other side of the tent wall, only a few centimetres from her head. She cringed away, remembering stories of wild wolves.

Then she remembered Moonbeam and relaxed. She must have escaped again and come looking for more cornflakes. Ellie just

needed to go outside and catch her. Then the noise would stop.

Suddenly, something scratched at the tent wall – something hard, something like a claw. There was no way a pony could make a sound like that. It couldn't be Moonbeam. It must be a wolf.

Ellie fumbled for her torch. Maybe light would drive the creature away. But in her panic, she knocked the torch over and it tumbled with a loud clang into a tin of hoof oil. Instantly, the snuffling stopped, and Ellie heard something crashing through the undergrowth.

Kate sat bolt upright in her sleeping bag. "What's happening?"

she asked, snapping on her torch.

"There's something outside," whispered Ellie. "I heard it snuffling round the tent. It was trying to scratch its way in." She paused for a moment. Then she added, "I think it was a wolf!"

Kate put her hands over her mouth in alarm and shrank down as if somehow being smaller would make her safer. They sat very still and listened. The only sound was their own breathing. Even the rain had stopped.

"I can't hear anything," whispered Kate.

"Neither can I," Ellie whispered back. "Perhaps it's run away."

"Unless you dreamed it," suggested Kate.

"I didn't!" declared Ellie. "I was as awake as I am now, and I promise you there was something there."

"But it couldn't have been a wolf," said Kate. "There aren't any wolves in the palace grounds."

"That's what everyone *thinks*," explained Ellie. "But just because nobody's seen one doesn't mean there aren't any here."

"That's true," said Kate. She shivered with fear and pulled the sleeping bag up to her chin. Then she dropped it again suddenly as her eyes opened wide with horror. "What about the ponies? What if the wolf's gone after them?"

Neither of them wanted to go outside. But their love for Moonbeam and Rainbow overcame their fear. They crept across to the pony shelter, holding hands to give each other courage. Kate carried the torch. Ellie was armed with the remains of the umbrella.

She didn't need it. There was no sign of the wolf, and the shelter looked exactly as it had when they left it. Moonbeam and Rainbow turned their heads to see who was disturbing their sleep. Their eyes glittered in the bright light of the torch.

Ellie hugged Moonbeam and pressed her face close to the pony's neck. The warm smell of horse was reassuring; it reminded her of

home. "Perhaps we could bring our sleeping bags over and sleep here," she said.

Kate shook her head. "There's not enough room. We'd end up being trodden on."

They lingered for as long as they could, stroking the ponies and shaking up their hay. But the cold seeped through their thin nightclothes and attacked their bare toes inside their boots. Soon they were shivering so much that they had to run back to the tent to get warm.

Kate dived into her sleeping bag and pulled it tight around her neck. "I suppose we could eat something," she suggested.

Ellie didn't reply right away. She was too busy battling with her nightdress as she wriggled into her bag. But once she was safely inside, she opened her backpack and pulled

out the food Kate's gran had packed for them.

Nestling underneath it was the phone the King had given her. Ellie bit her lip nervously as she stared at it. All she had to do was make one call and they'd be whisked back to safety and warmth at the palace. But that would mean admitting her father was right – that she couldn't cope with the freedom of being on her own.

Ellie fastened the backpack and pushed it away. Then she passed Kate a chunky bar of chocolate and kept one for herself.

This wasn't how she had imagined a midnight feast. She had pictured them sitting out under the stars feeling happy, not curled up in their sleeping bags, cold and scared.

They ate in silence, listening for any more strange sounds. But the creamy chocolate helped them feel better. When they'd finished, they settled down to sleep again. Neither of them wanted to creep out into the darkness to clean their teeth.

"They won't go rotten in one night," declared Kate.

Ellie happily agreed. But when she lay down to sleep, the silence seemed scarier, the night darker, and the ground even harder than before. She tossed and turned for what seemed like for ever. But eventually she dozed.

*

When she woke up, sunlight was streaming into the tent. It made everything look warm and friendly again, and drove away her fear. She was tired after such a disturbed night and so was Kate. Reluctantly, they crawled out of their sleeping bags and threw on clean clothes.

Ellie was glad they'd fetched some water the night before. She didn't fancy walking to the stream that early in the morning. But as soon as she put her finger in the bucket, she pulled it straight out again. "It's freezing," she said. "Do you want to wash first?"

Kate felt the water and shook her head. "I don't think I want to wash at all. We aren't *very* dirty, are we?"

Ellie suspected they were, but she wasn't going to argue. She was too busy regretting turning down the offer of hot water. "Let's see to the ponies before breakfast."

"What breakfast?" said Kate. She picked up the remains of the cornflakes packet and tipped out the few remaining flakes. "Thanks to *your* pony we've got nothing to eat."

Ellie was feeling irritable after so little sleep. "What do you mean – *my* pony," she snapped. "They're both *my* ponies." She regretted the words as soon as she'd said them.

Kate's eyes filled with tears. "That's right. Rub it in. It's not *my* fault I haven't got a pony of my own. *My* parents aren't rich like yours.

Mine can't afford to buy me everything I want."

"I'm sorry," mumbled Ellie. But it was too late. The damage was done.

Kate turned away and stormed out of the tent.

Chapter 7

Ellie ran after Kate, determined to put things right. She found her in the pony shelter, crying into Rainbow's mane. As soon as Ellie arrived, Kate straightened up and wiped away her tears with her hands. Then she grabbed a dandy brush and began to groom the grey pony as if nothing was wrong.

Ellie followed her lead and started

brushing Moonbeam. "At least it's stopped raining," she said, in an attempt to lighten the atmosphere.

Kate ignored her.

"And we can ride all day," Ellie continued.

Kate still said nothing.

"And I really am sorry," said Ellie, with much more sincerity than she had the first time. "I didn't mean to hurt you."

Kate gave a silent shrug and concentrated on Rainbow's mane.

Ellie was nearly in tears herself. Kate was her best friend. They'd never fallen out before, and she wasn't sure she wanted to spend all day riding with someone who wouldn't speak to her. It was a relief when the Range Rover arrived.

Although it was morning, Higginbottom was still wearing his evening suit. Ellie realized she had never seen him in anything else and she wondered if he went to bed in it too.

He bowed as he handed her two packed lunches for later in the day. Then he coughed politely and said in an embarrassed voice, "I know that is all you requested, Your Highness, but Cook refused to listen to me." He opened the back of the car and lifted the cover from one of the two silver trays that lay

inside. "She insisted I brought this, just in case, but I'm happy to take it back if you wish."

Ellie's mouth watered at the sight of sausages, bacon, eggs and hot, buttered toast. "You might as well leave it," she said, trying to hide her delight.

"It would be such a shame to see it go to waste," added Kate, as she peered over Ellie's shoulder. "And I wouldn't like to offend my gran."

Ellie and Kate grinned at each other and Ellie knew she was forgiven. They tucked into their breakfast together and the hot food cheered them up, giving them the energy they needed to tackle the morning chores.

As they cleared away the manure and fetched fresh water, they kept their eyes open for signs of the mysterious creature. But there weren't any. The short grass was too springy to show paw prints, and the snapped twig Ellie found beside the tent *might* have been there when they arrived.

By the time they set out on their ride, Ellie had nearly forgotten how frightened she had been in the night. It was wonderful to be back in the saddle and to have a whole day to enjoy by themselves. Moonbeam and Rainbow seemed as excited as their riders. They tossed their heads and kept trying to jog instead of walking.

Meg must have spent ages planning the treasure hunt. When they opened the envelope she'd given them, Ellie and Kate

found a map with the route marked on it, questions about the places they would see on their way, and a list of animals and birds to look out for as they went along.

"We've got to spot a deer, a squirrel, a blackbird, a crow, a robin and a pheasant," read Kate.

"And we start by going back the way we came yesterday," said Ellie, who was in charge of the map.

She read out the first question:

"Through the wood
to the giant pine.
How many hollies
stand in line?"

"I remember that tree," squealed Kate. "Come on! Let's get started."

Soon both girls were completely absorbed in the game. Meg had planned the route to make riding fun. There were tiny paths to explore, small logs to jump and wonderful long stretches of grass to canter across. The questions were perfect too – not too easy and not too difficult. The animal-spotting was the hardest part. All the creatures were well camouflaged and wary of visitors. It took sharp eyes and patience to find them.

Ellie felt blissfully happy as she rode along. This was how camping should be – just like in her book. If only it could always be this good. If only there wasn't another night to get through; another night when the mysterious creature might come back to get them.

Chapter 8

It was late in the afternoon when Ellie and Kate rode down a wooded slope towards a wide stream.

"We've nearly finished," said Kate. "And we've only seen the birds so far."

"Don't worry," said Ellie. "There's still time." She pulled Moonbeam to a halt beside a fallen log and read the last but

one verse on her sheet:

"Find the log and look up high.

Whose home is that against the sky?"

They peered up into the branches of the nearby tree where they could just catch sight of a tangle of twigs.

"What sort of bird lives there?" wondered Kate.

Then a movement caught their eye. A red squirrel scampered into view, sprang onto another tree and disappeared behind the trunk.

"That's it," said Ellie, triumphantly. "It's a squirrel's drey."

"And we can cross *squirrel* off the spotting list," added Kate. "So we've found everything now, except the deer."

"We might still see some," said Ellie.

Kate shook her head. "I think they're too shy."

Ellie read the last verse. This one wasn't a question. It was an instruction.

"Across the stream and past the tree

Back to camp in time for tea."

"That sounds like a good idea," said Ellie with a yawn. "I'm tired and the ponies must be too." She urged Moonbeam into the stream they had to cross, but the palomino hesitated at the edge, peering nervously at the water.

"I'll go in front," said Kate. "Rainbow's hardly frightened of anything." She rode past Ellie and the grey mare stepped happily into the stream.

"Good girl, Moonbeam," said Ellie, as the palomino followed close behind.

The stream was deepest in the middle. The water reached above Rainbow's knees and that's where the grey pony decided to stop. Kate urged her on, but Rainbow took no notice. Instead, she started to paw at the water with a front hoof, sending cascades of droplets over her squealing rider.

"Stop it," pleaded Kate.

Ellie giggled. "She thinks you should have washed this morning."

At that moment, Rainbow stopped splashing. She started to lie down instead.

"No!" yelled Kate. She kicked the pony with her heels but it made no difference.

Ellie tried to help. She rode up to Rainbow and leaned forward to try to grab the pony's bridle. But she couldn't reach it in time. The grey pony sank down into the

stream with a sigh of satisfaction.

Kate jumped off and screamed as the ice-cold water soaked through her jodhpurs. Ellie roared with laughter. It was the funniest sight she'd seen for ages.

Suddenly, there was a crashing in the undergrowth beside the stream. Two terrified deer shot out of the bushes and raced away.

The noise frightened Moonbeam. She leaped sideways in an attempt to escape, and the sudden movement took Ellie by surprise. She was still leaning forward, and she was laughing so much that she wasn't concentrating on her riding. Before she could do anything to save herself, she lost her balance and slid over the palomino's shoulder. With a huge splash, she landed flat on her back in the water.

It was Kate's turn to laugh. "Now we've both had a bath. And we've finally seen a deer."

"I wonder what frightened them," said Ellie, as she struggled to her feet.

"Us laughing, I suppose," suggested Kate. She looked more serious and added, "Unless..."

Ellie bit her lip nervously. "Are you thinking what I'm thinking?"

Kate nodded slowly.

"The wolf!" they both said at once.

Chapter 9

Ellie shivered as they rode hurriedly back to camp. The sun was too low in the sky to give much warmth and her wet clothes gave her no protection from the chill breeze. But it wasn't just cold that was the problem. She was scared too. The deer's fear had triggered her own, and brought back memories of last night's mysterious visitor.

As they reached the top of the hill, she caught a glimpse of the palace in the distance. It looked warm and welcoming. She thought longingly of hot showers and soft, fluffy towels, but she didn't say anything. She didn't want Kate to think she was a wimp.

Their camp looked cold and unfriendly in comparison, but it felt good to get out of the wind. They quickly unsaddled the ponies and gave them their hay. Then Ellie and Kate ran to the pink tent to get changed. It smelled dreadful inside. The spilled milk had gone off in the warmth of the afternoon, and it stank.

Kate wrinkled her nose in disgust, as she struggled out of her wet jodhpurs. "That's what we get for not clearing it up," she groaned.

Ellie had never thought of doing that, or picking up yesterday's clothes, or straightening her sleeping bag. No wonder her half of the tent looked such a mess. She was so used to having servants around that she'd never realized how untidy she was.

She pulled off her wet clothes and dumped them in a reasonably tidy heap. Then she rubbed her arms and legs briskly with a towel to try to bring some warmth back into them. Thank goodness it was nearly suppertime. Some hot food was just what they both needed.

Unfortunately, it wasn't what Higginbottom brought. Kate's gran had provided smoked salmon salad, crusty bread and lashings of ice cream. She probably thought it was the ideal meal for the end of a sunny day.

"It would be much warmer at home," said Kate. She pulled her coat tightly round her as she sat outside nibbling her lettuce. They didn't want to eat in the smelly tent.

Ellie looked at her in surprise. "Are you feeling homesick too?"

Kate nodded. "Just a bit."

"But you've been camping lots of times," said Ellie.

"Not on my own, I haven't," said Kate. "I've always had my mum and dad with me

before." She paused and looked nervously round at the surrounding trees. "And there aren't any wolves in the desert."

Ellie knew exactly what she meant. The cold and the damp and the smell were only part of the problem. Although she didn't like them, she was sure she could cope if she tried hard enough. But wild animals with big teeth were another thing altogether. Surely her father wouldn't make fun of her for running away from one of those.

"We could go home now if you wanted," she suggested. It wouldn't look so bad if Kate gave up first.

"No," replied her friend. "We'll manage. There's only one more night."

"And the wolf probably won't come back," added Ellie, with more confidence

than she felt. She pulled the phone out of her backpack and slipped it into her coat pocket. That would make it easy to find in the night because she intended to sleep in her coat to keep warm. If the mysterious visitor returned, she was going to call the palace right away.

When bedtime came, they rearranged the tent so that their sleeping bags were right next to each other. Then they put the ponies' saddlecloths over their pillows in the hope that the lovely horsey smell would hide the disgusting smell of sour milk. They wriggled into their sleeping bags and snuggled close together. But the ground was still hard and Ellie's mind was racing with scary thoughts. So she was wide awake when the mystery visitor returned.

Ellie's stomach churned with fear as she listened to the snuffling. There was only a thin layer of tent material between her and the creature outside. Her imagination went wild, picturing sharp teeth and claws tearing at the fabric.

She reached over to wake Kate, but she didn't need to. Her friend was already alert and listening. She took Ellie's hand and squeezed it reassuringly. At least they were both in this together.

The snuffling, snorting noises moved along the outside of the tent until they reached the doorway. Suddenly the sound stopped and the tent flap moved. The two girls huddled closer together, terrified of what might happen next.

But the only thing that came through the gap was a sliver of moonlight. It shone on Ellie's backpack that lay where she had dropped it, just inside the entrance.

Then the backpack began to move.

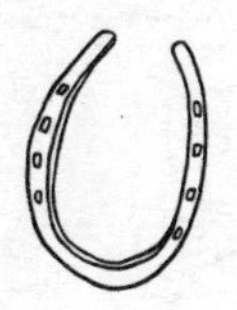

Chapter 10

Ellie stared in amazement as the backpack slid slowly out of the tent. What on earth would a wolf want that for?

She tugged Kate's arm and pointed towards the entrance. In the dim light from the moon, she saw her friend nod and start to crawl silently out of her sleeping bag. Ellie did the same. Very, very quietly, they crept forward

and peered under the tent flap. Their mystery visitor had its nose deep in the backpack.

"It's a deer," whispered Ellie, in surprise. Although she spoke as quietly as she could, her voice was loud enough to startle the animal. He pulled his head out of the backpack and stared at them in alarm. His antlers looked magnificent silhouetted against the moonlit sky, but the grand sight was lessened by one of Ellie's socks dangling from his mouth.

The two friends stayed so still that they hardly even dared to breathe. It was wonderful to be so close to a wild deer. They didn't want to scare him away.

But at that moment, there was a sound of movement behind the tent. It wasn't the quiet pad of paws, or the light feet of another deer. This was the unmistakeable thud of hooves.

Ellie's heart sank as she saw Moonbeam wander into sight. The palomino pony had escaped again and she had chosen exactly the wrong moment to come searching for more cornflakes.

But the deer didn't run away. Instead, he turned his head to look at Moonbeam and, for the first time, Ellie noticed that his left ear drooped sideways.

The two girls looked at each other and both silently mouthed, "Stanley."

He wasn't a fawn any more. He was a fully grown stag. But Kate's grandad had been right. Stanley definitely wasn't as timid as

other deer. He stood completely still as Moonbeam walked up to him. Then he dropped the sock and sniffed noses with her.

The presence of another animal seemed to give Stanley extra confidence. He turned his attention to the backpack again. This time he had help. Moonbeam nuzzled it too.

"What are they after?" asked Kate in a low voice.

"I bet it's my peppermints," Ellie whispered back. She reached into her jacket pocket and pulled out another packet. Then she crept out of the tent, holding out a peppermint on the palm of her hand. She was too excited to care that her feet were bare and the grass was damp with dew.

Stanley stepped back as Ellie came towards him. He kept close to Moonbeam's side, then his nose twitched as he smelled the scent of peppermint on the air. So did Moonbeam's. She reached out and took the sweet as soon as Ellie was close enough.

Ellie tossed another one to Stanley. It landed just in front of him and he picked it up happily. Then he came forward looking

for more. Kate gave him the next one. She popped it on the ground beside the tent.

As the deer bent to pick it up, one of his antlers touched the pink material. It made a familiar scratching sound – one that Ellie remembered from the night before. "So it wasn't claws at all," she said.

"But I don't blame you for thinking it was," Kate replied with a grin. Then she glanced at her watch. "It's midnight. Just the right time for a feast."

They spread blankets on the damp grass and wrapped themselves in their sleeping bags. Then they sat outside in the moonlight and munched chocolate cake and crisps.

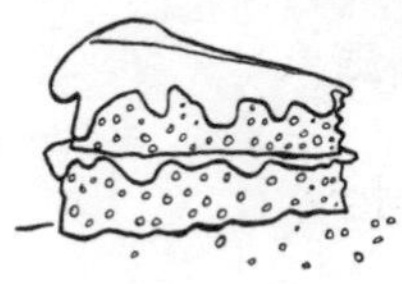

Moonbeam and Stanley grazed happily

beside them while, above them, thousands of stars twinkled in the velvety sky.

Ellie reached into her pocket and pulled out the mobile phone. "I don't need this," she said, and tossed it into the tent. She felt so happy here, with Kate, and the ponies and Stanley. The King had been completely wrong. Camping really was fun.

Pony-Mad Fun & Facts

Dear Reader,

Are you as pony-mad as Princess Ellie? I am. I've loved ponies for as long as I can remember. But I didn't get the pony I dreamed of until I was grown up.

When I was a child, I had to make do with reading about ponies and making up imaginary stories about them. Maybe that's why I write pony books now.

I hope you enjoy Princess Ellie's adventures and, because I remember how much I loved learning about ponies, there are some fantastic facts and fun quiz questions just for you in the following pages...

Love,

Diana

xx

Meet Princess Ellie's ponies

Moonbeam

MOONBEAM

You've read all about
Moonbeam's talent for escaping –
now find out a little bit more about her...

COLOUR: Palomino – a golden coat with
a white mane and tail.

SPECIAL TRICK: Wriggling out of her
headcollar.

LIKES: Cornflakes

DISLIKES: Umbrellas

ABOUT MOONBEAM: Moonbeam is a
gentle pony, but she can be nervous
and she sometimes bucks. She is
good friends with Rainbow.

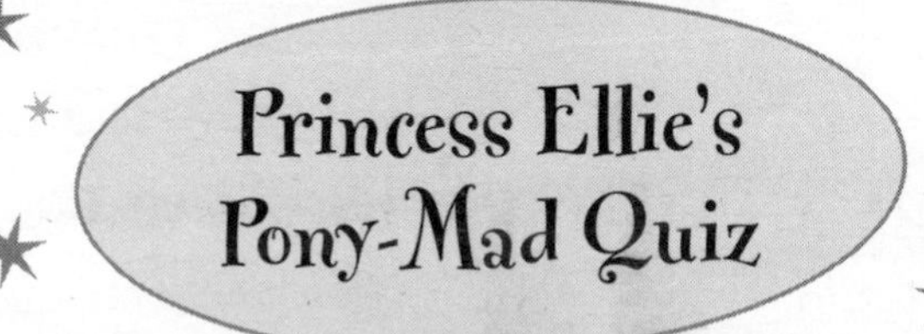

Princess Ellie's Pony-Mad Quiz

Do you know your stirrup from your saddle? Or the name of Ellie's Shetland pony? Test your knowledge of Princess Ellie's world with this quiz!

1. Ellie and Kate feed the lambs:

a) Orange juice

b) Water

c) Milk

2. When going riding, you should always wear:

a) A riding hat

b) A cowboy hat

c) Your crown

3. What did Miss Stringle give Ellie for the camping trip?

a) Chocolate biscuits

b) Pencils and paper

c) Maths homework

4. Which decorations were on Ellie and Kate's tent?

a) Silver moons and stars

b) Pink rosettes and horseshoes

c) Gold bows and crowns

5. The size of a pony is measured in:

a) Metres

b) Hands

c) Feet

6. A "girth" is used to:

a) Protect the horse's back

b) Attach the stirrups to the saddle

c) Hold the saddle in place

7. Ponies swish their tails around to:

a) Swat flies

b) Annoy other horses

c) Show they are happy

Turn the page to find out the answers...

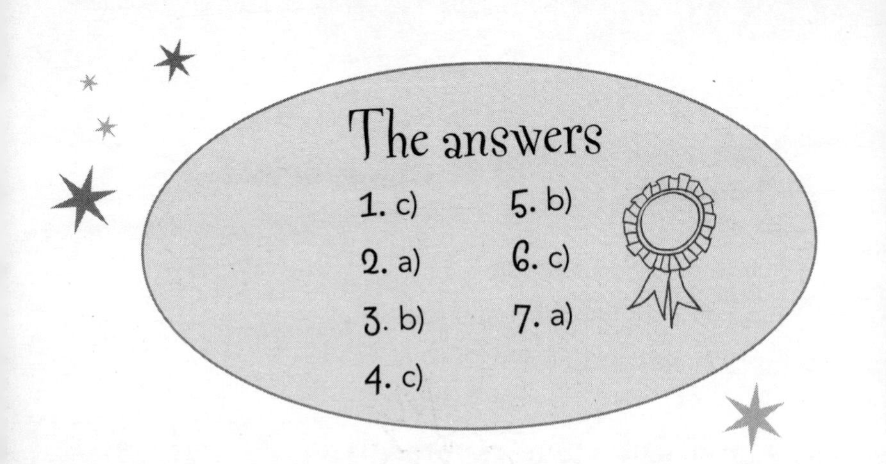

The answers

1. c)
2. a)
3. b)
4. c)
5. b)
6. c)
7. a)

Tot up your total to see just how pony-mad you are...

1-3
A good try.

4-6
Great knowledge and a big rosette!

7
You are totally pony-mad – it's a **gold cup** for you!

How to...
Camp like a princess

Kate and Ellie know it's very important to take all the right things for a camping adventure. Here are their top tips!

* It can get very chilly at night in a tent, even during the summer, so always make sure you pack lots of blankets, jumpers, a woolly hat and big socks!

* It's good to check the weather forecast beforehand and always pack a rain jacket, just in case...

* Always remember to take a torch – it can get very dark at night without any other lights. It's also fun to use when telling stories!

* Remember to look up! You should be able to see lots of stars at night. Can you can spot the Milky Way, or Orion's Belt?

* Put something between the groundsheet and your sleeping bag to stop the cold coming up from the ground while you are asleep. An airbed, camp bed or camping mat all work well.

* If you're going on any walks, or just fancy a nutritious snack, mix together peanuts, dried fruit and a few chocolate treats to make the perfect combination to nibble on!

* Remember to store your snacks, cakes and sweets in a tin – you don't want to wake up and find any ponies or deers tucking into your treats!

Read on for a sneak preview of Princess Ellie's next adventure...

Chapter 1

"Good girl," said Princess Ellie, as she cantered Moonbeam towards the last jump. The palomino pony eyed the wooden poles warily and tried to swerve away. But Ellie was ready for her. She kept a firm hold on the reins and pushed the pony on with her legs. Moonbeam did as she was told. She leaped forward and cleared the jump easily.

Ellie galloped between the finishing posts and pulled her pony to a halt. Then she turned round to see how the others were getting on.

She was just in time to watch her best friend soar over the wooden poles on Rainbow. Kate's jumping had improved enormously since she came to live with her gran, the palace cook. Perhaps that was because of all the practice she had on Ellie's ponies.

Prince John was further back, riding Sundance. The chestnut pony jumped over a fallen tree trunk and cantered down the hill towards the last obstacle. Then he pricked his ears forward, lifted his front legs and bounded over it. Prince John grinned broadly. It was hard to tell which of them was enjoying themselves most, as they galloped through the finishing line.

"That was brilliant," said John, as they rode slowly back towards the stables. "I'm going to ask my father to build a cross-country course in the grounds of *our* palace – but I'm sure mine will be longer."

"Of course it will," sighed Ellie. She really liked John. He was the only royal person she knew who shared her love of ponies. But he did have an annoying habit of insisting everything was bigger and better at his home in Andirovia.

Kate leaned forward and patted Rainbow's grey neck. "I'm not surprised you want one," she said. "Cross-country's much more exciting than jumping in the paddock."

"But even that's not as exciting as a real adventure," said John. "Do you remember how we went hunting for ghosts last time I came to stay?"

"I was really scared," said Ellie.

"So was I," agreed Kate.

"But it was still fun," laughed John. "What are we going to look for this time?" The girls stared at him blankly. "Well, aren't there any mysterious legends about your palace? What about tales of hidden treasure?"

"I've never heard any," said Ellie.

"Dragon's eggs?" asked John.

"Now you're being silly," giggled Kate.

"How about a secret passage, then?" suggested John. "All the *best* palaces have one of those. Our one at home is brilliant."

"But that's not secret," Ellie declared with delight. "It can't be if *you* know about it."

At that moment, they reached the lane that led to the palace stables. A bay pony whinnied loudly and cantered across the nearby field to meet them. She was larger than the ponies they were riding, and the long hair that nearly hid her hooves made her look like a miniature carthorse. She skidded to a halt beside the fence and put her head over the top rail.

"This is Starlight," explained Ellie, as Moonbeam sniffed noses with the bay pony. "Do you like her?"

"She's lovely," said John. It was the first

time he had come to stay since Starlight arrived, so he hadn't met her before. "She looks much better than she did in that photo you emailed to me."

Ellie smiled proudly. "I'd only just found her then. She'd been living wild for so long that she looked really neglected."

"She doesn't any more," said John. He twisted a finger thoughtfully in Sundance's chestnut mane and added, "She's quite fat now."

"No, she's not," said Ellie, indignantly. "She's just well built. Ponies like her have big bones." She turned Moonbeam firmly away from the fence and led the way towards the stables. "You don't have to be thin to be beautiful."

There was a long, awkward pause. Then Kate broke the silence by saying, "Wasn't Ellie clever to catch Starlight?" She looked wistful for a moment and added, "I wish I could find a pony."

"So do I," said John. "I'd like a palomino, like Moonbeam."

"Copycat!" cried Ellie.

"No, I'm not," said John. "My palomino would be bigger than yours."

"Then it wouldn't be like Moonbeam, would it," Ellie declared. "Anyway, you don't need another pony. You've got two already." She'd seen plenty of pictures of the beautiful, chestnut mares he'd left behind in Andirovia.

"Why shouldn't I have three?" argued John. "*You* already had Sundance, Moonbeam, Rainbow *and* Shadow when you got Starlight. That's five." He sighed and shrugged his shoulders. "Anyway, there's no point arguing about it. My father already thinks I spend too much time riding.

There's no way he'd buy me another pony."

"My dad won't get me a pony at all," added Kate, very quietly.

The sadness in her voice made Ellie feel guilty. It was mean of her to argue with John about how many ponies they had, when Kate didn't even have one. Ellie was happy to share her ponies with her best friend, but she knew that wasn't the same. Kate desperately wanted a pony of her own. If only there was something Ellie could do to help.

To find out what happens next read

A Surprise for Princess Ellie

Princess Ellie to the Rescue ISBN: 9781409565963
Can Ellie save her beloved pony, Sundance, when he goes missing?

Princess Ellie's Secret ISBN: 9781409565970
Ellie comes up with a secret plan to stop Shadow from being sold.

A Puzzle for Princess Ellie ISBN: 9781409565987
Why won't Rainbow go down the spooky woodland path?

Princess Ellie's Starlight Adventure ISBN: 9781409565994
Hoofprints appear on the palace lawn and Ellie has to find the culprit.

Princess Ellie's Moonlight Mystery ISBN: 9781409566007
Ellie is enjoying pony camp, until she hears noises in the night.

A Surprise for Princess Ellie ISBN: 9781409566014
Ellie sets off in search of adventure, but ends up with a big surprise.

Princess Ellie's Holiday Adventure ISBN: 9781409566021
Ellie and Kate go to visit Prince John, and get lost in the snow!

Princess Ellie and the Palace Plot ISBN: 9781409566038
Can Ellie's pony, Starlight, help her uncover the palace plot?

Princess Ellie's Christmas ISBN: 9781409566045
Ellie's plan for the perfect Christmas present goes horribly wrong...

Princess Ellie Saves the Day ISBN: 9781409566052
Can Ellie save the day when one of her ponies gets ill?

Princess Ellie's Summer Holiday ISBN: 9781409566069
Wilfred the Wonder Dog is missing and it's up to Ellie to find him.

Princess Ellie's Treasure Hunt ISBN: 9781409566076
Will Ellie find the secret treasure buried in the palace grounds?

Princess Ellie's Perfect Plan ISBN: 9781409556787
Can Ellie find the perfect plan to stop her best friend from leaving?

Check out more sparkly stories at
www.usborne.com/fiction